Unicorn Magic

Dawnblaze
Saves Summer

To Ida Mason

Special thanks to Conrad Mason

ORCHARD BOOKS

First published in Great Britain in 2019 by The Watts Publishing Group

1 3 5 7 9 10 8 6 4 2

Text copyright © 2019 Working Partners Limited
Illustrations © Orchard Books 2019
Series created by Working Partners Limited

A CIP catalogue record for this book is available from the British Library.

ISBN 978 1 40835 692 0

Printed and bound in Great Britain by Clays Ltd, Elcograf S.p.A

The paper and board used in this book are made from wood from responsible sources.

Orchard Books
An imprint of Hachette Children's Group
Part of The Watts Publishing Group Limited
Carmelite House
50 Victoria Embankment
London EC4Y 0DZ

An Hachette UK Company
www.hachette.co.uk
www.hachettechildrens.co.uk

Contents

Aisha and Emily are best friends from Spellford Village. Aisha loves sports, whilst Emily's favourite thing is science. But what both girls enjoy more than anything is visiting Enchanted Valley and helping their unicorn friends who live there.

Dawnblaze

Dawnblaze is the Fire Unicorn. She loves to swim in the hot springs on Firework Mountain with her dragon friends!

The Air Unicorn, Shimmerbreeze, is in charge of making sure the air in Enchanted Valley is fresh and clean. She likes to use her magic to create little breezes, so her friends can fly their kites.

Shimmerbreeze

Glitterhoof

Glitterhoof is the Earth Unicorn, who makes plants grow strong and beautiful. What she likes best is being part of a team – there's nothing she won't do for her friends!

Sparklesplash has so much fun playing in the rivers and lagoons of Enchanted Valley. This Water Unicorn wants everyone to love the water, just as much as she does.

Sparklesplash

An Enchanted Valley lies a twinkle away,
Where beautiful unicorns live, laugh and play
You can visit the mermaids, or go for a ride,
So much fun to be had, but dangers can hide!

Your friends need your help – this is how you know:
A keyring lights up with a magical glow.
Whirled off like a dream, you won't want to leave.
Friendship forever, when you truly believe.

Chapter One
A Horse in the Attic

"I can't believe we're really going to live here!" said Aisha Khan. She stared up at her new house, clutching a cardboard box full of her belongings.

Enchanted Cottage had a thatched roof, neat little windows and walls the colour of summer sunshine. The front garden was bursting with red and blue flowers. A rose bush grew on either side of the doorway, spreading over it in a leafy green and pink canopy.

Aisha's dad threw an arm around her shoulders. "Home, sweet home!" he said.

"It's perfect," said Aisha, grinning.

The Khans walked up the cobbled path, and Aisha's mum got out the keys. The front door was bright red, with a silver door knocker. It was shaped like a horse's face, with a single silver horn on its forehead.

"A unicorn!" said Aisha's mum, fitting the key in the lock. "I never noticed that before."

The door creaked open, and Aisha raced up the stone stairs to find her bedroom.

The summer sun shone through the window on to the old floorboards.

The slanted ceiling had wooden rafters, and there was a soft, cosy bed in the corner. Through the window, Aisha could see the big green lawn of the garden. In the middle was a statue of a magical bird, flying out of a fire. A phoenix, her dad had called it.

She put her box down on the bed. Inside were a tennis racket, swimming goggles, a cricket ball and a big collection of football stickers. Aisha loved sport more than anything.

Just then, the doorbell rang. "I'll get it!" shouted Aisha, and she raced down the stairs.

When she opened the door, she found a girl about her age standing before her.

The girl was wearing a stripy T-shirt, shorts and trainers. Her hair hung loose and curly round her shoulders.

"Hi!" said the girl. "I found a football on the road outside." She held it out. "I thought it might be yours."

"Oh, thanks!" said Aisha, taking the ball. "It must have fallen out of the removal lorry."

"I'm Emily Turner, by the way," the girl said. "I haven't seen you before!"

"We've only just moved to Spellford," said Aisha. "I'm Aisha Khan."

Emily looked around the front garden in awe. "I wondered who was moving into Enchanted Cottage. I've always wanted to see what it's like inside!"

"Why don't you stay for a bit?" said Aisha, smiling. "We can explore the cottage together!"

Emily clapped her hands with excitement. "I'd love to!"

Aisha led Emily through to the kitchen. Her mum and dad were unpacking pots and pans, and Aisha introduced them to Emily.

"It's lovely to meet you, Emily!" said Aisha's mum.

"How about we make some tea and get the biscuits out?" said her dad.

"Thanks!" said Aisha. "And I'll show Emily the cottage."

Aisha's mum smiled. "You girls have fun exploring the place. We'll call you when it's time for tea."

The two girls raced upstairs to Aisha's room.

"Let me guess," said Emily, picking up Aisha's tennis racket. "You really love sport!"

"That's right!" said Aisha with a grin. "What's your favourite hobby?"

"Science!" said Emily. "I love it. I've got a science kit at home with test tubes and safety goggles." She grinned back. "But I love magic too. That's why I always thought Enchanted Cottage looked so cool. You know, with the unicorn knocker and everything."

"Me too!" said Aisha. From somewhere above, they heard a distant thumping. Emily frowned. "What was that?"

"It sounded like … hoofbeats!" said
Aisha.

They both listened hard. Again, the
thumping sound echoed above them.

They stepped out on to the landing. A
ladder stood at one end, going up into
darkness above. Emily shivered. "There

can't be a horse in the attic, can there?" she said.

"Come on," said Aisha, stepping on to the bottom rung of the ladder. "There's only one way to find out!"

Chapter Two
Queen Aurora

"I can't see a thing!" said Aisha, as Emily climbed up into the attic after her.

"If we wait, our eyes will get used to the dark," said Emily.

Sure enough, as they stared into the darkness, they began to see piles of dusty cardboard boxes, and an old sofa with the stuffing falling out.

Aisha frowned. "There definitely isn't a horse up here!"

"So where did the hoofbeats come from?" wondered Emily.

"Whoa!" Aisha crossed the attic to a low table beside the sofa, making the floorboards creak with each step. "Look at this!"

Emily went to join her. Sitting on the table was a little glass model. It was twinkling despite the dim light.

"It's a unicorn!" cried Aisha.

Emily carefully picked it up. The unicorn fitted perfectly in her palm. It had a delicate crystal horn, and its two front hooves were raised. Even in the darkness,

the unicorn glittered.

"What colour is it?" asked Emily. "It's hard to tell."

Aisha glanced around for a light switch and spotted a skylight covered over with a blind. She stepped on to an old stool, stretched up on tiptoes and pulled a cord.

Swish! The blind flew open and beams

of sunshine flooded through the window into the attic. The girls blinked and covered their eyes from the bright light.

When Emily looked again, she gasped.

In the sunshine, the girls could see swirls of colour glowing inside the unicorn, in every colour of the rainbow. The colours swirled faster and brighter. Then – *whoosh!* – they exploded around the unicorn in a shower of sparkles, like a firework going off.

The girls gasped as the sparkles flew around them, whirling past so quickly their feet were lifted off the floor.

"We're flying!" said Emily, as a blur of colour whizzed past their faces.

Suddenly the sparkles disappeared, and

the girls drifted on to solid ground.

Aisha looked down at their feet. They were standing on soft grass. "This can't be right!"

"What happened?" said Emily. "Where are we?"

"I've no idea," said Aisha. "But I don't think we're in the attic any more!"

Emily pointed up ahead. "Aisha, look!"

On a hillside stood a glittering golden palace. Flowers climbed up the walls, swaying slightly in the breeze, and windows glinted in the sunlight. The palace had lots of tall turrets rising against a bright blue sky.

"They look like unicorn horns!" said Aisha in amazement.

"It's incredible," Emily whispered. "What is this place?"

Aisha shivered with excitement. "Let's find out!"

Hand in hand, the girls walked up the grassy hill towards the palace. The higher they climbed, the further they could see. Beautiful meadows, forests and lakes stretched out all around them. Fluffy clouds floated above, and the girls glimpsed winged creatures darting in and out of them.

"I don't think those are ordinary birds," said Emily, staring up in wonder.

Aisha shook her head. "This place is amazing!"

When the girls reached the top of the hill, they saw that the palace was surrounded by a moat of crystal-clear water. A silver drawbridge swung down over the moat, chains clinking as it fell into place.

Then, trotting out over the bridge, came a unicorn.

Her mane and tail were shining gold, and her body was the colour of the dawn – pink one moment, then red the next … then orange, then gold … The colours seemed to come and go, like clouds

flitting across a sky. On the unicorn's head was a delicate silver crown.

"I can't believe it! She looks just the model in the attic!" said Emily.

The unicorn stopped at the end of the drawbridge. She swished her tail, then bowed her head at the girls. Her golden horn sparkled in the sunshine.

"Hello, girls!" said the unicorn. Her voice was soft and gentle.

"You can speak!" gasped Emily.

The unicorn gave a laugh that sounded like sweet music, and tossed her mane. "I certainly can! My name is Queen Aurora. Welcome to Enchanted Valley!"

Chapter Three
Extravaganza!

For a moment the girls didn't know what to say. Then Aisha bowed low. "Hello, Your Majesty," she said. "I'm Aisha Khan."

"And I'm Emily Turner," said Emily, curtseying. "We love your palace!"

"Thank you!" said Queen Aurora.

"Why don't you come inside?" With a swish of her tail, she trotted back across the drawbridge.

"I don't understand. How did we get here?" whispered Aisha.

"I can think of only one explanation ..." said Emily.

"Magic!" the girls said at the same time. With that, they held hands and followed Queen Aurora into the palace.

The unicorn led them through a gate and into a courtyard, where ivy-covered walls surrounded them. More unicorns trotted across a neat green lawn. In the middle of the grass, two silver unicorns were admiring a delicate paper chain hanging around a stone fountain that

was shaped like a leaping dolphin. Three
green-and-blue unicorns walked over
with little lanterns hovering beside them.
The lanterns settled in the branches of the
orange trees that grew around the edge of
the courtyard.

"What are they doing?" Emily asked.

"They're getting ready for a party," Queen Aurora said. "At the end of the week, we are holding our Nature Gala. We have it every summer! All our friends from Enchanted Valley are invited. The gnomes, the imps, the griffins … and the dragons, of course!"

"Dragons?" said Aisha, exchanging a wide-eyed look with Emily. "This place is amazing!"

Queen Aurora beamed with pride. "Come and see the kitchen. Our unicorn chefs are making party food!"

She trotted across the courtyard, and the girls followed. As they passed, each unicorn dipped its horn.

"That's how unicorns wave to each

other," explained Queen Aurora.

The girls dipped their heads to wave back.

Queen Aurora led them through a long, white stone corridor, down some steps and into a huge kitchen. It had a roaring fire and bronze pots and pans hanging from the ceiling. Several unicorns wearing chefs' hats were hard at work.

"Mmmm," sighed Emily and Aisha, breathing in the scents of vanilla, chocolate and cinnamon. The kitchen was full of the most delicious baking smells!

A pale blue unicorn wearing a chef's hat stood at an oven. He smiled at the girls before turning his gaze to a round

tin filled with cake mixture. He dipped his horn towards the tin, as if it were a magic wand, and sparkles surrounded it.

Swooosh! All at once, the mixture turned a pretty blue.

"More magic!" whispered Emily.

"Oh yes," said Queen Aurora. "Magic is what makes everything work in Enchanted Valley. Do you see what's hanging around his neck?"

The girls saw that the chef unicorn

wore a little crystal locket, hanging from
a delicate golden chain.

"The lockets give us our magic," said
Queen Aurora. "And we use them to look
after Enchanted Valley. Each unicorn has
a different kind of power." She lifted her
head, and Emily and Aisha saw that she
had a locket too.

"Mine is the Friendship Locket," Queen
Aurora explained. "I protect all the
friendships in Enchanted Valley."

Aisha carefully lifted
up the locket for a
closer look. Through
the clear glass, she
and Emily could see
two tiny golden suns

floating around each other. They looked like a pair of friends playing.

"It's beautiful!" said Aisha.

Queen Aurora flicked her tail. "There are so many beautiful things in Enchanted Valley ... and in Enchanted Cottage, too!"

Emily gasped. "How do you know about the cottage?" she asked.

"Let me show you," said Queen Aurora. She led them out of the kitchen and down a grand corridor filled with vases of flowers. At the end was a wide staircase. Aisha and Emily followed Queen Aurora up the softly carpeted stairs and into a long white hall. Sun shone in through windows on one side, and on the other hung a row of large portraits. Some of the paintings were very old, with dusty golden frames. But there were newer ones too. Each one showed a pair of children in front of the palace.

The first was an oil painting of a girl and a boy wearing velvet tunics and frilly white collars. In another, a pair of boys were wearing smart jackets and ties. Aisha studied a painting of two girls in floor-length dresses.

"Who are all these children?" she asked.

"All the boys and girls in these portraits once lived in Enchanted Cottage," said Queen Aurora. "And they all found their way here, to Enchanted Valley. You see, there is a magical connection between the two places."

"Wow," sighed Emily. "We're so lucky!"

"I'm glad you think so," said Queen Aurora. "And we're lucky that you two came to visit!" She smiled, and her golden mane sparkled in the sunshine. "Now, let's meet the nature unicorns! They're in charge of the party."

Queen Aurora trotted under an arch at the end of the hall, into a sunny garden.

The girls came out after her and gasped. The garden was even prettier than the courtyard they'd first seen. It had lush green grass, colourful flowerbeds and a sparkling stream leading to a pool full of water lilies.

Four unicorns were gathered at a big,

round table with a white tablecloth. A
long scroll was laid out on top, and the
unicorns were looking at it and chatting
excitedly.

"That's their party plan," whispered
Queen Aurora. Then she called out,

"Hello, friends! Come and meet our visitors!"

The four unicorns looked around at Queen Aurora's call, then trotted over, swishing their tails happily.

As a red unicorn with a bright orange mane and deep brown eyes came closer, the girls saw tiny little fireworks exploding and glittering in her locket. "I'm Dawnblaze," she said. "I'm the fire unicorn! I keep Enchanted Valley lovely and warm."

"And I'm Shimmerbreeze, the air unicorn!" said a white unicorn. Her locket was full of miniature fluffy clouds. "I keep the air clean."

"I'm Glitterhoof, the earth unicorn,"

said a green unicorn, whose locket had a flower in it. "I make sure the flowers and plants can grow."

"And I'm Sparklesplash," said a deep blue unicorn, with a fountain in her locket.

"You must be the water unicorn!" said Emily.

"That's right!" said Sparklesplash. "I protect the water of Enchanted Valley."

Aisha grinned. "It's so lovely to meet you all!"

The unicorns grinned back, looking at Aisha and Emily in wonder. It was as if the girls seemed magical to them!

Just then, a cold wind swept through the garden. It ruffled the unicorns' manes and

blew the scroll on to some bushes. The girls shivered. Dark clouds covered the sun and threw the garden into shadow.

Aisha felt a spot of rain on her head. Then another. Then down it came in a great shower.

The girls huddled together under one of the orange trees as the rain soaked their clothes.

"That came on fast!" said Emily.

Queen Aurora tossed her damp mane out of her eyes. "Oh dear," she said anxiously. "We should get inside, and "

But before she could finish, lightning streaked through the sky. *Boooom!* Thunder rolled loudly, sounding like a whole herd of galloping horses.

With a flash of silver, another unicorn
leaped over the palace wall. She landed
on all four hooves in the garden. But this
unicorn didn't seem like the others. Her
silver body shone like the moon, and her
mane and tail were twilight blue. She had
purple eyes, and as she glared around,
both girls felt a flutter of fear.

Emily gasped. "Who is that?"

Chapter Four
Selena's Big Moment

Queen Aurora's eyes were open wide, and her ears stood up with fright.

"It's Selena!"

The other four unicorns cowered behind their queen, frisking their tails anxiously.

"Surprise!" cackled the silver unicorn. She reared up, waving her hooves in the

air. Electricity
sparked over her
body. Then a
bolt of lightning
shot from her
horn. *Fffzzzappp!*
A nearby rose
bush burst into flames, frazzled by her
magic.

The girls ducked, holding on tightly to
each other.

"Look!" said Aisha suddenly. She
pointed at a glass locket hanging from
Selena's neck. Inside it was a little black
storm cloud, with a lightning flash inside.

"Uh-oh," said Emily. "She must have
made this storm with her magic!"

Just then, a furry
little black ball came
swooping down over the wall. It rolled
across the grass and sprang into the air,
fluttering a pair of silky wings.

"It's a bat!" cried Aisha.

"Here I am, Your Majesty!" said the bat,
bowing in mid-air to Selena. "Sorry I'm
late. I got really lost, and—"

"Silence, Flit!" roared Selena, stamping
her hoof. "You're spoiling my big
moment!"

She turned back to Queen Aurora. "So,
we meet again," she sneered. "Except
this time, I have a plan to take over the
Golden Palace, and rule over the whole
Valley!"

"Leave us alone, Selena!" cried Dawnblaze.

"Aurora is our queen, not you," added Sparklesplash.

"Not for long!" snapped Selena. "You see, I'm going to steal the powers from every unicorn and use them to take over Enchanted Valley ... starting with you four!"

Selena whipped her horn from side to side. Suddenly a great wind swept into the garden, tearing rose petals from the bushes and swirling them around in circles.

Then the wind snatched up the four lockets of the nature unicorns. *Clink!* Four silver chains were lifted off the unicorns' heads, and the lockets went whirling through the air. Queen Aurora jumped up to catch them, but with a whoosh they zoomed past her and landed around Selena's neck.

"Oh no!" cried Emily.

"Give us back our lockets!" said Shimmerbreeze, pawing at the ground.

Selena cackled. "Oh, I will," she promised. "Just as soon as you make me the queen of Enchanted Valley! Give me the crown, or you'll never see your precious lockets again!"

There was another flash of lightning

and a *BOOM* of thunder. Emily and
Aisha clutched each other tightly. Then
Selena flew off into the sky, her silver
body shimmering in the rain.

"Wait for me!" puffed Flit. He went
fluttering after her, and they disappeared
among the dark clouds.

Dawnblaze hung her head in despair.
"Oh no," she said. "This is our fault – we
were so excited to meet you both, that we
forgot to be on guard against Selena."

"What are we going to do?"
Sparklesplash said. "We can't let Selena
become queen! She'll turn Enchanted
Valley into a horrible, scary place."

Emily and Aisha moved closer to
Dawnblaze and stroked her mane, trying

to cheer her up. Then, suddenly, the rain stopped. But just as the girls thought the sun might come out again, they felt the air getting colder. The tips of the grass went white with frost, and the pool turned to ice. A freezing wind blew through the garden.

"What's happening?" asked Aisha, shivering.

"It's because my magic is gone!" said Dawnblaze. "With my locket, I kept Enchanted Valley nice and warm. But now Selena has it, her magic will reverse the locket's power, and make the opposite happen. Instead of being warm, everything will freeze. It will be winter for ever!"

"I won't let that happen," said Queen Aurora. "I'll go and get the lockets back!"

"But you're the queen!" said Glitterhoof. "If you're not guarding the palace, Selena might try to take it over!"

"Then let us go," said Aisha, taking Emily's hand. "We'll find the lockets."

Emily gave Aisha's hand a squeeze and nodded. "Starting with Dawnblaze's," she added.

The unicorns all turned to look at them. Queen Aurora flicked her tail anxiously. "I'm not sure, girls," she said. "It's very kind of you ... But Selena will try to stop you. It could be dangerous."

"We're not scared of her," said Aisha.

Aurora nodded. "Very well, then," she said. "But you must at least stay warm." Her horn glowed a deep orange, and the air sparkled with magic. When the girls looked down, they were astonished to see that over their summer clothes they were wearing cosy snowsuits, with furry hoods, thick gloves and boots.

"And I'll go with you," said Dawnblaze. "Just jump on my back."

"Thank you,

girls!" said the other unicorns together, as Dawnblaze kneeled down for the girls to clamber up on to her back.

"You are true friends," Queen Aurora added. "Good luck, and be safe!"

Aisha held on tight to Dawnblaze's fiery mane, and Emily sat behind her. Then the unicorn trotted forward. "Here we go!" she cried.

The girls gasped in shock as Dawnblaze galloped through the garden. Then – *whoosh!* – she leapt into the sky, flying up and over the palace wall.

Chapter Five
Firework Mountain

"You can fly!" cried Aisha.

"Of course!" laughed Dawnblaze. "All unicorns can!"

Emily glanced back and saw the Golden Palace getting smaller and smaller, until it looked no bigger than a toy castle. She felt a shiver of fear. "We're

very high up!" she murmured.

"Just hold on to my waist," said Aisha,
gripping Dawnblaze's mane. "I won't let
us fall."

Emily wrapped her arms around Aisha,
and at once she felt calmer.

As they flew, the girls gazed around
them in wonder. From up here they
could see Enchanted Valley, laid out like
a grassy green carpet beneath them.

A sparkling river ran near the Golden
Palace, and all around were thick, dark
forests, green meadows and castles.

Emily gasped as a flock of golden-
tailed creatures swept beneath them.
"Phoenixes!" she cried. "Those must
have been the creatures we saw flying in
the clouds!"

"Wow!" breathed Aisha. "They're just
like the statue in Enchanted Cottage!"

The wind roared in their ears and stung their eyes. Suddenly, they felt little cold pinpricks on their faces. "Snowflakes!" cried Emily. Sure enough, white flecks of snow were swirling and drifting around them.

"Oh dear," said Dawnblaze anxiously. "We must get my locket back soon – or it will never be summer again!" She shuddered. "If it gets much colder, the underwater creatures will be trapped under ice, and all the flowers will die … It will be terrible!"

"Where do you think Selena has taken the locket?" wondered Aisha.

Emily frowned. "Her magic makes your locket have the opposite effect, right?"

"That's right," said Dawnblaze.

Emily tried to think like a scientist. She peered all around, narrowing her eyes against the snow falling through the air. The cold seemed to be spreading out from a place in the far distance — a mountain. The top of it was white with snow, and ice lay on the slopes.

"See over there?" she said, pointing.

"That's Firework Mountain," said Dawnblaze. "It's a volcano. Usually it's lovely and warm there, but now it looks freezing!"

"It's where the cold's coming from," said Emily, "so I think it's where the locket must be. It must be what's made the volcano freeze."

"Nice one, Emily!" said Aisha. "Let's go!"

Dawnblaze whinnied with excitement and they soared towards the mountain.

As they flew, the wind howled louder, whirling the snowflakes in every direction. Aisha and Emily tightened their grip, clinging on for dear life.

When at last Dawnblaze swept over Firework Mountain, the girls looked down and saw a big crater at the top of it. Inside was a frozen pool of ice.

"I can't believe it!" said Dawnblaze. "Normally the volcano shoots out sprays of colourful sparks, like fireworks. But now everything is frozen! Even the dragons have gone. They're friends of mine, and we love to swim in hot pools on the mountain

slopes ..." She looked
down below them.
"But those are all
frozen too!"

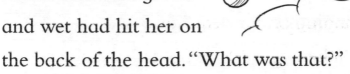

"Ooof!" gasped
Aisha. Something cold
and wet had hit her on
the back of the head. "What was that?"

"I think it was a snowball!" said Emily,
wiping snow off Aisha's hood.

"Oh no ..." said Aisha, pointing to a
black spot in the sky. "It's Flit!"

The little bat flapped out from behind a
cloud, with two more snowballs clutched
in his claws. "Take that!" he squeaked,
and threw one at Emily.

Emily dodged it, but she leaned over

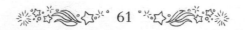

too far and lost her balance. "Woah!" she cried, slipping from Dawnblaze's back.

"No!" cried Aisha. She reached down to catch Emily's hand, but it was already too late — she was tumbling off the unicorn.

Flumph! Emily landed softly in a snowdrift beside the crater. She wiped snow from her face and sat up, smiling. "I'm all right!" she called. Then she spotted something glinting in the icy pool below. "Over here!" she cried.

Dawnblaze swooped down and landed gently in the snow at Emily's side.

Aisha climbed down off the unicorn's back, feeling a little dizzy. She wobbled and held on to some rocks at the edge of the pool.

Peering into the icy water, the girls saw something small, trapped in the ice and glowing with a hundred different colours.

"It's the locket!" cried Emily.

"And we only found it because of Flit!" said Aisha, grinning. "If he hadn't thrown snowballs, we would never have spotted it."

"I bet he was probably trying to keep us away from the locket," Emily said. "But his plan backfired big time!" She waved

at the bat, still fluttering above. "Thank you!"

"Oh, drat!" yelped Flit. He flapped his wings and darted off through the falling snow.

Dawnblaze frowned, swishing her tail. "But how can we get the locket out?"

"Leave it to me!" said Aisha. She picked up a big rock from the side of the pool and crouched down by the ice. She used the rock like a hammer … but it was no good. The ice didn't crack. She tried again and again, but the rock barely made a dent. At last Aisha put the rock down. "This isn't working," she sighed. "What now?"

Emily thought hard. "I know!" she said at last. "If we can't break the ice, we'll have to melt it! Then we can fish out the locket."

"That could work!" said Aisha. "But we'd need a lot of heat." She frowned, but then her eyes brightened with an idea. "Dawnblaze, do your dragon friends breathe fire?"

Dawnblaze tossed her mane with excitement. "They do! That's a great idea! I'll call them now." The unicorn stamped her hoof three times and gave a whinny that sounded like bells chiming.

A moment later, three huge, glittering

creatures came diving out of the clouds. The girls stared in wonder as the dragons looped the loop, their tails streaming behind them.

"I've never met a dragon before," said Emily, her eyes wide.

"Me neither!" said Aisha.

"They're very friendly," Dawnblaze promised.

The dragons landed all together and folded their big, shiny wings. Up close, Emily and Aisha saw that they were as big as buses, with kindly blue eyes. They were shivering in the cold. Frost lay across their backs, and snowflakes gathered on their eyelashes.

"Hello, dragons!" said Dawnblaze.

"These are my friends, Aisha and Emily."
She turned to the girls. "This is Sparky,"
she said, nodding at the first dragon,
which was gold. "And these are Smoky
and Coal." She nodded at the silver
dragon, then the bronze one.

"H-h-hello, Dawnblaze!" said Smoky,
his teeth chattering. "Have you come to

make it w-w-w-warm again?"

"We're trying!" said Dawnblaze. "But Selena has frozen my locket in there." She pointed to the crater with one hoof.

"That n-n-naughty Selena!" said Sparky. "Now our toasty home is f-f-frozen!"

"Will you help us stop her?" asked Aisha bravely.

The bronze dragon called Coal looked at Aisha. "Yes, little h-h-human. What can we do?"

"Can you melt the ice with your breath?" asked Emily.

"W-w-we'll certainly try," said Smoky. "W-w-won't we?"

The other two dragons nodded. They

stretched out their long necks like giraffes, until their heads were just above the icy pool. Then together, they breathed …

Phut!

Three little gusts of snowflakes blew out and settled on the ice.

"It's no good!" said Smoky sadly. "We're so cold, we don't have any f-f-fire left in us!"

The girls' hearts sank. Without fire, there was no way they could melt the ice.

"I have an idea," said Dawnblaze. "There is someone who could warm up the dragons. But I haven't seen him in a very long time. I'm not sure if he'll help us."

"Anything's worth a try," said Aisha.

"Can you take us to him?"

Dawnblaze stamped the snow with her hooves. "Hop on!" she said.

Chapter Six
Stinky Potion

"Who are we going to see?" asked Emily, as they flew down the mountainside through the falling snow.

"His name is Hob," said Dawnblaze. "He's very old and very wise. And he's a goblin! He lives near here."

"I hope he'll help us!" said Aisha.

Dawnblaze swooped down into a forest. Here and there, the tops of trees poked up through the snow. She looked around, stamping her hooves. "That's funny," she said. "I'm sure his home was around here somewhere …"

Just then, the girls heard something.

"What was that?" asked Aisha.

"It sounded like someone calling for help!" said Emily.

They looked around, puzzled. Then the cry came again.

"I think it's coming from under this snow!" said Aisha.

Quickly the girls climbed off the unicorn's back and began to dig. Dawnblaze helped, using her front hooves to shovel snow aside.

"Look!" cried Aisha, scraping away
an armful of snow. Beneath it was the
dark opening of a cave. The snow had
completely covered it.

"Help!" cried the voice again, louder
now.

A light shone from inside, then a funny
little creature appeared, holding an old-
fashioned lantern. He wore a long purple
gown and a
pointed hat
with silver stars
on, and his face
was green and
wrinkly. He
wasn't much

more than half as tall as Aisha and Emily.

"This is Hob!" said Dawnblaze.

"Oh dear me, thank you!" squeaked the little creature. He pushed a pair of gold spectacles up his nose. "I was worried I'd never get out from under all that snow!"

"Don't mention it," said Emily. "Pleased to meet you."

"I'm Aisha, and this is Emily," said Aisha. "We've come to ask for your help!"

"Hmm," said Hob thoughtfully. "I don't

get many visitors … and you did dig me out. Very well – come in!"

Hob hurried off down a large, dark tunnel, humming to himself. Dawnblaze and the girls followed.

The tunnel led into a big cavern. Lanterns and crystals glittered from the ceiling. There were wonky wooden shelves propped up on the rocks, and every one of them was crammed with little pots and bottles full of strange ingredients.

Emily peered at the containers, but she didn't recognise anything from her science books. "What's Gossamer Glitter?" she asked.

"And what's Comet Dust?" wondered Aisha.

"Ingredients for my potions!" said Hob, rubbing his hands together.

"Actually, that's why we came," Dawnblaze said. "Could you help us make a potion?" She quickly explained what had happened.

"So you see, we need the dragons to melt the ice so we can get my locket back," Dawnblaze finished. "But they've become so cold, they're breathing snow instead of fire!"

"Dear me, what a pickle," said Hob, straightening his hat. "Let's warm up those dragons! I'll get my potion pot bubbling away. You two can fetch the ingredients."

Hob began calling out instructions as he placed a blackened pot over the fire. "Two pints of forest dew, please! And four ounces of spider silk!"

Aisha raced around, finding the ingredients, while Emily measured them out and put them in the pot.

"Very good!" said Hob, watching Emily mix in some silver dust.

"She's a natural!" said Aisha.

Emily blushed. "It's just like a science experiment," she said. But as she was

reaching for a bottle of liquid rainbows, a black shape darted from the shadows and snatched it away. "Oh!" she gasped. "It's Flit again!" cried Aisha.

Sure enough, Selena's bat flapped around the cave, holding the bottle in his claws. Aisha snatched at him, but he just flew higher. "It's mine now!" he squeaked in triumph. "You'll never finish your stinky potion!"

"He must have sneaked in after us," said Emily. "What do we do now? We can't reach him!"

Just then, the cave filled with a warm,

dazzling light. Turning, the girls saw that it came from Dawnblaze's horn. It was glowing like a torch.

"Gah!" squawked Flit. "Bright light!" He tried to cover his face with his wings, and he dropped the bottle. Down it fell, towards the rocky floor …

Thump! Just in time, Aisha dived and caught it. She curled up, holding the bottle tightly, like a goalkeeper with a football.

"What a save!" yelled Emily.

Hob snatched up a broom and jabbed it at Flit. "Out, you naughty creature!"

Squeaking crossly, Flit darted down the tunnel and disappeared.

"Whoa, that was close!" said Aisha.

 79

"You did it, Dawnblaze!"

The unicorn stamped at the ground, looking pleased.

Hob quickly mixed the liquid rainbows into his potion pot. Then he took a glass flask from inside his robe and spooned the potion into it. It was thick and purple, and smelled very strange, like sour milk mixed with rotten bananas.

"It tastes better than you'd think," promised Hob, as he handed Aisha the flask. "Now, good luck, girls! All the creatures of Enchanted Valley are counting on you!"

Chapter Seven
Icy For Ever

Outside, the wind howled and the snow
pelted down as Dawnblaze leaped into
the air, Emily and Aisha holding tightly
to her back. But the wind drove her down
into the snow again. "Oh no!" puffed
the unicorn. "I can't fly in this terrible
weather."

"We'll just have to walk," called Aisha, over the roar of the wind. "We need to save Enchanted Valley!"

The girls and Dawnblaze started to struggle up the side of the mountain. The crater seemed a very long way off.

Emily stopped, panting. "I don't know if I'll make it," she said sadly.

"This won't do," said Dawnblaze. "But the dragons can carry you!"

"Not you?" Emily asked.

Dawnblaze shook

her head. "Unicorns don't mind being ridden, but we don't make very good riders! I know you girls will find a way to get the locket."

She stamped her hoof three times and whinnied. But no dragons came swooping through the snow.

"Where are they?" wondered Dawnblaze.

"I bet they didn't hear," said Emily. "This wind is too loud!"

"What if we all stamped together?" said Aisha.

"Good idea!" said Dawnblaze. "Are you ready? Now!"

The girls stamped their feet, and Dawnblaze stamped her hooves. Then

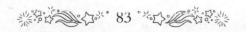

Dawnblaze whinnied and the girls whistled as loudly as they possibly could.

They peered into the falling snow, but there was nothing but whiteness all around.

Dawnblaze hung her head. "I don't think it worked."

But just then, three shining creatures came swooping from behind a cloud.

"It's the dragons!" shouted Emily.

Sure enough, Sparky, Smoky and Coal came gliding down towards them.

"Hello there!" boomed Smoky, as they landed – *whumph!* – in the snow.

"Looks like you need our h-h-help," said Sparky between his shivers. "C-c-c-climb on. We'll get you back to the crater in

n-no time!"

Emily and Aisha looked nervously at each other. But there wasn't a moment to lose. Aisha climbed on to Smoky, and Emily climbed on to Sparky. Their scales were freezing cold, and not nearly as comfortable to sit on as Dawnblaze's soft, warm hair. But the girls clung on as tightly as they could.

"I'll wait with Hob," said Dawnblaze. "Good luck, girls!"

Then with a great whoosh, the dragons soared up into the sky. Emily and Aisha could feel the massive wings moving beneath them as they flew closer and closer to the mountaintop.

In a few moments they came gliding

down to land by the crater. Dawnblaze's locket was still there, buried deep in the ice.

The girls slid to the ground. Aisha brought out the flask, and Emily poured a few drops into each dragon's mouth.

"It tastes y-y-yummy!" said Coal.

"But did it work?" asked Aisha anxiously.

The girls held their breath, waiting. But the dragons looked just as cold and shivery as before.

Then all of a sudden, something strange began to happen. Woolly hats appeared on the dragons' heads, made of glowing golden light. Then came thick golden scarves, wrapping around their necks.

"I feel warm!" cried Smoky.

"Me too!" agreed Coal.

"This is much better!" said Sparky. "All together now. One … two … three!"

The dragons all breathed down on the crater.

WHUMPH! Three huge bursts of flame roared across the ice. Aisha and Emily gasped and stumbled back at the sudden heat. A great cloud of steam rose into the air. The girls saw chunks of ice breaking apart, and water bubbling beneath.

As the steam cleared, the girls peered anxiously into the pool. The locket was free! But now it was sinking fast through the water, out of reach and getting further and further away ...

"Uh-oh!" gasped Aisha.

"If we don't get it back, summer will be lost for ever!" said Emily. "What are we going to do?"

"I'm going in!" yelled Aisha. She took off her magical snowsuit, boots, and gloves, so she was dressed in her leggings and vest again.

"Be careful!" Emily cried.

Aisha took a deep breath, ran and jumped.

SPLASH! She plunged deep into the water. The locket was below, the silver chain trailing as it sank …

Kicking her legs, she snatched hold of it. Then she swam upwards, holding her breath until she burst out into the air again.

Emily grabbed Aisha's arms and pulled her out. "You did it!" she cried. "Are you OK?"

Aisha nodded, shivering. "I'm f-f-freezing, though!"

Quickly, Sparky passed Emily her glowing scarf, and Emily draped it around Aisha's shoulders.

A warm glow spread through Aisha, and all the water vanished from her clothes. "Wow!" she gasped. "I'm dry!"

"Phew!" said Emily, helping Aisha put her snowsuit and boots back on. "You were so brave! Now we just need to get the locket back to Dawnblaze."

"Climb on," said Coal. "We'll have you there in no time!"

Chapter Eight
True Friends

They soon arrived at Hob's home. Emily
and Aisha hurried through the tunnel to
find Dawnblaze and Hob waiting by the
fire in the cavern.

"What happened?" asked Dawnblaze,
her eyes wide. "Did you manage to get
my locket back?"

Aisha grinned and held the locket up. Dawnblaze let out a whinny of excitement, and Aisha hung the locket back around the unicorn's neck.

At once, Dawnblaze's horn began to glow. A fiery redness spread across her mane and tail, and her eyes sparkled. She tossed her mane and rubbed her nose against Aisha and Emily's cheeks. "Thank you, girls!" cried the unicorn.

"You did it!" said Hob, dancing a little

jig. His glasses fell off, but he didn't seem to mind.

Back outside, the girls couldn't believe their eyes. The sun had come out again, and the ice and snow were melting. They could see grass and rocks appearing everywhere as the slush melted away.

"Summer is saved!" sighed Dawnblaze happily. Emily and Aisha grinned, shrugging off the winter clothes Queen Aurora had given them. The sunshine felt lovely on their skin.

"Look at Hob's home!" gasped Emily.

Aisha turned to look, and she saw that the entrance to the goblin's home wasn't a cave at all. It was a gap in the trunk of a huge old oak tree, which had been

completely covered by snow.

"And just you wait, girls," said Dawnblaze. "Here comes the best bit!"

Whhhhhsshh! Zzzzzzzipp! Booooom!

The girls spun round and stared in amazement. Gigantic sparks were shooting out of the top of Firework Mountain. Reds, golds and yellows shimmered in the sky, as though it was an open box of firecrackers.

"It's amazing!" sighed Aisha.

The dragons flew up in the air, soaring
and flicking their tails with delight.
"Hurrah!" they cried. "Our home is
warm again!"

But just then, someone came flying
round the side of the mountain. The girls'
hearts sank. *Selena!* And Flit was with her,
flapping desperately to keep up.

"You human pests!" screeched the silver
unicorn. She landed on a rock, stomping
her hooves with fury. "You think you can
stop me? I've still got three lockets, you
know. The unicorns will make me queen!"

Flit landed beside Selena. "What did
I miss?" he gasped.

Selena rolled her eyes. "Everything!" she
snapped. Then she took off again, darting

away across the sky. Puffing and panting, her little bat followed.

"She's right," said Dawnblaze. "She still has three lockets. We have to get them back."

"And we will!" said Aisha.

Emily nodded. "We promise."

Soon afterwards, Dawnblaze was gliding down towards the Golden Palace, with Aisha and Emily riding on her back. The girls grinned as they looked around at the valley, all green and summery once again beneath a clear blue sky.

As soon as Dawnblaze landed in the garden, Queen Aurora and the other Nature Unicorns galloped up to them.

"You did it!" said Aurora, beaming

as Dawnblaze's locket shimmered in the sunlight. "You're true friends of the unicorns! And now that summer is saved, it's time to celebrate."

Everyone cheered. The pale blue unicorn brought out the cake he had baked earlier. They all gathered around the table to eat it. The cake had chocolate icing and rainbow-coloured sprinkles. It was rich and fudgy, and the most delicious thing Emily and Aisha had ever tasted. It was almost like there was magic baked in …

"Selena can't stop us from enjoying ourselves," said Dawnblaze.

"The Gala must go ahead," said Queen Aurora. "No matter what!"

Aisha finished her slice of cake and
sighed. "I wish we could stay here for
ever."

"Uh-oh!" said Emily, her stomach
dropping. "That reminds me ... my
parents! They've probably been looking
everywhere for us!"

"Don't worry," said Aurora, shaking her
head. "Whenever you are in Enchanted
Valley, no time passes in your world. You

will return exactly when you left. Even so, it's probably time I got you girls home. You've done so much today."

"But what about the other lockets?" asked Aisha.

"You'll know when it's time to come back to the Valley," said Aurora mysteriously. "For now, goodbye, girls. And thank you!"

Emily and Aisha threw their arms around Aurora's neck and hugged her tight. Her golden mane was soft against their skin.

Then Aurora's horn began to glow and sparkle. Sunshine spilled out of it, swirling around and around, until all Emily and Aisha could see was a bright golden light.

Whhhhooooosh!

Thump!

Emily and Aisha sat down heavily.
The Golden Palace was gone. They were
sitting on wooden floorboards, back in the
attic at Enchanted Cottage. Sunbeams
shone through the skylight.

Aisha checked her watch. "Aurora was right!" she said. "It's the exact same time as when we left."

"I just knew the cottage had some secrets!" said Emily. "But I never imagined anything like Enchanted Valley!" She smiled at Aisha. "And I never imagined I'd find such an amazing friend here."

Aisha hugged Emily tight – and caught sight of something floating up from the table by the sofa. It was the little crystal unicorn. "Look!" she gasped.

Right before their eyes, the unicorn turned gently in the air, glimmering with a thousand different colours. Then – *bang!* – it exploded in a shower of sparkles, just like the top of Firework Mountain.

Emily and Aisha blinked. When they looked again, there were two tiny unicorns floating in mid-air, each with a shining silver keyring attached.

Silently, the girls reached out and each took a unicorn.

"Do you remember what Aurora told us?" asked Emily, as she attached her unicorn to a belt loop.

"She said we'd know when it was time to come back," said Aisha. She tucked her keyring into her waistband. "I have a feeling that somehow, these little unicorns are going to tell us when."

"Then we'd better always wear them," said Emily.

The voice of Aisha's dad floated up to them from downstairs. "Aisha! Emily! Your tea's getting cold!"

"Should we tell your parents about Enchanted Valley?" asked Emily, as they climbed down the ladder from the attic.

Aisha laughed. "I don't think they'd believe us, even if we did! It can be our secret."

The girls grinned at each other.

"When do you think we'll go back?" Emily wondered.

"Really soon, I hope," said Aisha. "I can't wait to see some more unicorn magic!"

The End

Join Emily and Aisha
for another adventure in …
Shimmerbreeze and the Sky Spell
Read on for a sneak peek!

Aisha Khan pointed up at the sky. "Look!" she said with a grin. "There's an elephant!"

Aisha and her best friend, Emily Turner, were lying on the lawn of Enchanted Cottage, watching the fluffy clouds float past – and spotting the ones shaped like animals. Aisha and her parents had moved to Spellford Village just a few days ago, and the two girls were already close. Together they had explored Enchanted Cottage – and discovered that the old thatched house held a wonderful secret …

"Aren't the clouds pretty?" said Emily. "Did you know that they're made of tiny droplets of water?" Emily loved science, just as much as Aisha loved sport.

"Cool!" said Aisha. Then she gasped. "Look at that one!" She pointed to where a large cloud was drifting over the top of the phoenix statue in the middle of the lawn. The cloud had a long tail and neck, and two great wings. It seemed to be pointing its tail down towards the outstretched wings of the magic bird below.

"Wow!" said Emily. "It's a dragon cloud!"

The girls shared an excited grin. On Aisha's first day in Spellford, they had found a beautiful crystal model of a unicorn in the attic of Enchanted Cottage. When a sunbeam had touched the glittering model, they'd been transported to Enchanted Valley, a wonderful kingdom ruled over by friendly flying unicorns, and full of other magical creatures, too – like goblins and dragons!

"I can't wait to visit the unicorns again," said Aisha with a sigh. She took out a crystal unicorn keyring from her shorts pocket. Queen Aurora, the unicorn ruler of the valley, had given matching keyrings to the girls and promised they'd return to Enchanted Valley very soon. Emily took her unicorn keyring out of her jeans pocket too.

Suddenly, the dragon cloud seemed to shimmer, then melted away – letting a beam of sunlight shine down on the girls. Their keyrings began to glow and sparkle like magical stars. "Is Queen Aurora calling us?"

Read
Shimmerbreeze & the Sky Spell
to find out what adventures are in store for Aisha and Emily!

Also available

Book One:

Book Two:

Book Three:

Book Four:

Look out for the next book!

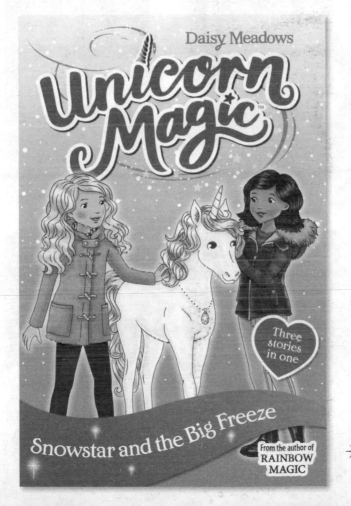

If you like
Unicorn Magic,
you'll love …

Welcome to Animal Ark!

Animal-mad Amelia is sad
about moving house, until she
discovers Animal Ark, where vets look
after all kinds of animals in need.

Join Amelia and her friend Sam for a
brand-new series of animal adventures!